First U.S. edition 2013

Library of Congress Catalog Card Number 2012942677

ISBN 978-0-7636-6430-5

SCP 17 16 15 14 13 12
10 9 8 7 6 5 4 3 2 1

Printed in Humen, Dongguan, China

This book was typeset in Baskerville.
The illustrations were done in watercolor.

Candlewick Press
99 Dover Street
Somerville, Massachusetts 02144

visit us at www.candlewick.com

For Reuben and James
S. S.

For Anton
R. B.

With thanks to
the Thornbury Vintage Tractor Museum,
the Geraldine Vintage Car Machinery Museum,
and Ted.
R. B.

Farmer John's Tractor

SALLY SUTTON   *illustrated by* ROBYN BELTON

CANDLEWICK PRESS

Farmer John's tractor lies locked in the shed,
rusty yet trusty and orangey red.

That winter, the rain comes. It rains and it rains.

It fills up the river and blocks up the drains.

The riverbanks break. It's a flood! Water swirls.

It rushes and gushes. It spurts and it twirls.

From down by the river, there comes a great shout:
"Help! Our car's stranded! We can't get it out!"

But Farmer John's tractor lies locked in the shed,
rusty yet trusty and orangey red.

From far down the road, a jeep's coming near.

It speeds through the water. The girls give a cheer.

But how could they guess what these deep waters hide?

A rock! With a splash, the jeep rolls on its side!

Along comes a tow truck, as strong as can be.

"Hold on," calls the driver. "I'll soon set you free!"

But look how the wheels spin around in the muck.

It sinks ever deeper—this tow truck is stuck!

The girls clamber onto the roof of the car.
The water's still rising. How frightened they are!

But Farmer John's tractor lies locked in the shed,
rusty yet trusty and orangey red.

A fire engine's coming! It's noisy and fast.

Its siren is wailing. Its horn gives a blast.

But it slams to a halt at the edge of the flood.

The rain's caused a slide! There are rocks in the mud!

The fire engine's useless. It has to reverse.

The crew's looking worried; the flood's getting worse.

Still Farmer John's tractor lies locked in the shed,
rusty yet trusty and orangey red.

The girls start to shake and to quake and to sob.

Surely there's someone who's up to the job?

What's this? Farmer John's by the shed with a key!

He unlocks the padlock. The tractor is free!

It grunts, then it splutters and starts with a roar,
and Farmer John's tractor chugs right out the door!
The girls see him coming, but how can they trust
this clanking old tractor, all covered in rust?

At last, Farmer John pulls up right by their side.

"Hop on! Squeeze together! Let's go for a ride!"

Mom and Dad cheer, and the girls shout, "Hooray!

Farmer John's tractor has just saved the day!"

They're safe and they're happy,
and free from all harm,
so Farmer John's tractor chugs back to the farm . . .

never again to be locked in the shed,
rusty yet trusty and orangey red.